David Almond writes:

'I grew up in a big family in a small steep town overlooking the River Tyne. It was a place of ancient coal mines, dark terraced streets, strange shops, new estates and wild heather hills. Our lives were filled with mysterious and unexpected events, and the place and its people have given me many of my stories.'

Four of the stories in *Where Your Wings Were* are also contained in the full-length collection *Counting Stars*, of which the critics wrote:

'This could well be Almond's best work yet.' *The Independent*

'*Counting Stars* is a moving, perceptive collection . . . These are sophisticated, serious tales . . . they are a wonder . . .' *The Times*

'This collection of short stories confirms Almond as a writer of compelling individual vision.' *The Scotsman*

David Almond's debut novel *Skellig* is one of the most remarkable children's novels published in recent years. It won the Carnegie Medal and was the 1998 Whitbread Children's Book of the Year. *Kit's Wilderness*, his second novel, was published to similar acclaim, winning both the Smarties Award Silver Medal and the Michael L. Printz Award. It was also highly commended for the Carnegie Medal and shortlisted for the Guardian Award. *Heaven Eyes* was shortlisted for both the Carnegie Medal and the Whitbread Award. *Counting Stars* and *Secret Heart* were both published to widespread acclaim.

Also by David Almond

Skellig
Kit's Wilderness
Heaven Eyes
Counting Stars
Secret Heart

Wild Girl, Wild Boy – A Play

David Almond

Where Your Wings Were

Hodder
Children's
Books

A division of Hodder Headline Limited

A Catalogue record for this book is available from
the British Library

ISBN 0 340 85527 4

Typeset by Avon Dataset Ltd, Bidford-on-Avon, Warks

Printed and bound in Great Britain by
Omnia Books Ltd, Glasgow

Hodder Children's Books
A Division of Hodder Headline Limited
338 Euston Road
London NW1 3BH

Contents

Introduction

These stories are about my childhood. They're about the people I grew up with, our hopes and fears, our tragedies and joys. They explore a time that has disappeared and a place that has changed. They bring back those who have gone, and allow them to walk and speak again within the pages of a book. Like all stories, they merge memory and dream, the real and the imagined, truth and lies. And, perhaps like all stories, they are an attempt to reassemble what is fragmented, to rediscover what has been lost.

The Middle of the World

She started with The Universe. Then she wrote The Galaxy, The Solar System, The Earth, Europe, England, Felling, Our House, The Kitchen, The White Chair With A Hundred Holes Like Stars, then her name, Margaret, and she paused.

'What's in the middle of me?' she asked.

'Your heart,' said Mary.

She wrote My Heart.

'In the middle of that?'

'Your soul,' said Catherine.

She wrote My Soul.

Mam reached down and lifted the front of Margaret's T-shirt and prodded her navel.

'That's where your middle is,' she said. 'That's where you were part of me.'

Margaret drew a row of stick figures, then drew concentric rings growing out from each of them.

'Where's the real middle of the world?' she said.

'They used to think the Mediterranean,' said Catherine.

'Medi means middle. Terra means world. The sea at the middle of the world.'

Margaret drew a blue sea with a green earth around it.

'There was another sea at the edges,' said Catherine. 'It was filled with monsters and it went right to the end of the world. If you got that far, you just fell off.'

Margaret drew this sea. She put fangs and fins for monsters.

'There's no end, really, is there?' she said.

'No,' said Catherine.

'And there's no middle, is there?'

Catherine laughed.

'Not really.'

Mam prodded Margaret's navel again.

'That's the middle of the world,' she said.

Later that day we went to the grave. Colin rushed home from Reyrolle's on his Vespa for lunch. He bolted his food and rattled away again. We heard the scooter taking him on to Felling Bank and down towards the square.

When it faded, Mary said,

'Should we go to the grave today?'

We hadn't been for months. We thought of the dead being in Heaven rather than being in the Earth.

'Good idea,' said Mam. 'I'll make some bara brith for when you get home.'

We were on the rocky path at the foot of the street when Dandy ran after us. He was a little black poodle that was never clipped and had horrible breath.

'Go home!' said Mary. 'Dandy, go home!'

He yapped and growled and whined.

'Dandy, go home!'

No good. We just had to let him trot along beside us.

Margaret fiddled with her navel as she walked.

'When I started,' she said, 'what was I like?'

'What do you think you were like?' said Mary. 'Like a gorilla? You were very very very little. You were that little, you couldn't even be seen. You were that little, nobody even knew you were blinkin there!'

'Daft dog,' said Catherine, as Dandy ran madly through a clump of foxgloves and jumped at bees.

Soon we saw Auntie Jan and Auntie Mona ahead of us. They wore head scarves and carried shopping bags on their arms.

'Bet you can't tell which is which,' said Mary.

'Even when they're talking to me I can't tell which is which,' said Margaret.

The two aunts hurried into Ell Dene Crescent.

'Did they look the same when nobody knew they were there?' said Margaret.

'Of course they did!' said Mary. 'Everybody looks the same when they can't be blinkin seen!'

The aunts waved and grinned and we all waved and Dandy yapped and then they hurried on again down into Ell Dene Crescent.

Mary picked daisies from the verges as we walked.

She said, 'Dad once said that daisies were the best of all flowers. I think I remember that.'

'You do,' said Catherine. 'You do remember. He called them day's eyes. Awake in the day and closed asleep at night.'

Further on, Daft Peter lay in his greatcoat under a tree on The Drive.

'Not him!' said Catherine. 'We'll never get away from him!'

We sat on a bench on Watermill Lane.

'How far is it?' said Margaret.

'You know how far,' said Mary.

'Nowhere's far in Felling,' said Catherine.

We watched Daft Peter.

'Move,' said Catherine. 'Go on. Move.'

'Is Felling very small?' said Margaret.

Mary stamped her feet.

'Yes,' said Catherine.

'Is it the smallest place in the world?'

'Is this Daft Question Day?' said Mary.

'Yes!' said Margaret.

'It's very small,' said Catherine. 'But there's smaller places.'

'Where?'

'Places in the desert,' said Mary. 'Rings of huts in the jungle. Villages in the Himalayas.'

'Yes,' said Catherine. 'And places like Hebburn or Seaton Sluice.'

'Not Seaton Sluice,' said Mary. 'It's got that big beach. It's got to be bigger than Felling. And Hebburn's got that big new shopping centre.'

Catherine sighed.

'Windy Nook, then,' she said.

'That's not fair,' said Mary. 'Windy Nook's a part of somewhere else.'

'Where, then? And make it somewhere we know.'

'Bill Quay,' said Mary.

No one said anything, even though we all knew Bill Quay was part of somewhere else as well.

'Thank goodness,' said Catherine. 'Bill Quay.'

Daft Peter didn't move. In the end, we walked on. Dandy snarled as we drew nearer to the man.

'Dandy!' said Catherine.

Daft Peter smiled and rubbed his eyes.

'Here's me thought I was dreamin,' he said. 'And all the time I'm just wakin up.'

He leaned against the tree.

'What would ye say if I knew how to turn swimmin fish into flyin fowl?' he said.

'Take no notice,' whispered Catherine.

'Nowt much at all, I see,' said Peter. 'But what if I said I could take you girls and show you how to fly aroond this tree.'

'I'd say you couldn't!' said Mary.

'Aha!' said Peter. 'Just let me look inside this bag, then.'

He dug into a brown carrier bag. He took out a sandwich, something bright red and black hanging out of two dried-out slices of bread. He held it out to Mary as we approached.

'Take a bite of that,' he said. 'Gan on, take a bite of that and see.'

Dandy jumped up at him, barking and snarling. Daft Peter flailed and kicked and the sandwich flew into the road.

'Daft dog!' he shouted. 'Look what ye've done to me dinna!'

We hurried past.

'What would ye say if I turned a daft dog into a nice meat pie?' yelled Peter.

'I'd say it would be very hairy and it would stink!' said Mary.

We arrived at the high steel graveyard gates. Just inside, withered flowers and broken wreaths were heaped in bins. Wasps and flies hovered and crawled. We held Dandy back from jumping at them. We all agreed that simple daisies were the best idea. We walked in single file on the narrow path between the graves. We murmured the names, the familiar and the unknown. At the far edge, just beyond the spiked fence, traffic thundered on the bypass.

We stood before our grave: *Barbara, beloved sister, 1959; James, beloved father, 1966; Neither can they die any more, for they are equal unto the angels*; and the empty area for other names. Mary placed the daisies by the headstone. We hung our heads and said our prayers. We said the prayers that Mam and Colin would have said. I imagined the two crumbled coffins and bodies, their intermingled dust. I imagined the new coffins being placed there, the new names being written, the new dust mingling. Not enough room to take all of us, not enough space for all of our names.

'What did she look like?' said Mary, as always.

'She was lovely,' said Catherine, as always. 'She looked a bit like all of us.'

'I love her,' said Margaret. 'And I never even saw her.'

'You remember Dad, though,' said Catherine. 'You can both see Dad.'

'Yes,' they said.

We dried our eyes and wandered among the graves. The untouched ground between the graves and the bypass was narrowing.

'Where will they *put* everybody?' said Mary.

Nobody knew.

'Maybe they go back to the start,' said Catherine, and we looked across the neat rows towards St Mary's church a quarter mile away, where the trees and the tilting faded gravestones were.

'It must have been lovely once,' Mary said. 'The little church and a few graves and none of the noise.'

As we walked back towards the gates, Margaret said,

'Are all the people here in Heaven like Dad and Barbara are?'

'Lots of them,' said Catherine.

'Heaven must be very big,' said Margaret.

'It must be blinkin enormous,' said Mary.

We walked through the stink of the flowers. Daft Peter waited outside against the graveyard wall. He swigged something from a black bottle.

We crossed the road and kept away from him.

'Have a sip of this!' he yelled. 'This'll get ye flyin!'

We heard the shuffle of his feet behind us as we turned on to The Drive. Dandy kept pausing, turning, snarling. Margaret kept on fiddling with her navel.

'Here!' yelled Peter. 'What would ye say if I said I knew where the entrance to Hell is?'

'I would say you were Daft Peter,' whispered Mary.

'What's that?' yelled Peter. 'What would ye say? Eh? Eh?'

Catherine sighed. She turned around. Dandy stood at her side, snarling.

'I'd say you were wrong and you don't and you should think more about the way up to Heaven. Now go away.'

Peter swigged from his bottle.

'Aha!' he said. 'Ahahaha! And what would ye say if I said if you went to Felling Square and went to the fountain and looked doon through the cracks in the pavements that ye'd soon get to feel the heat and smell the sulphur and see the fire and the Devil hisself waitin to welcome ye?'

Dandy snarled.

'Nowt much, I see,' said Peter. 'Cat got your tongues, eh?'

'It's not got mine,' said Mary.

'Nor mine,' said Margaret.

'That dog got me dinna!' he yelled.

Margaret giggled.

'Aha!' yelled Peter. 'And what would ye say if I said the top of that fountain's shaped just like a little lass's belly button?'

Margaret snapped her T-shirt down.

'Get him, Dandy!' said Mary, and Dandy rushed at Peter again. Peter kicked and flailed and his drink sprayed and splashed out of the top of the bottle. The dog trotted proudly back to us.

'There now,' said Mary. 'That's fettled him.'

8

'That dog got me dinna an me drink!' yelled Peter.

We giggled and sighed.

Auntie Mona came out of Ell Dene Crescent carrying her shopping bag.

'Just popping down for some bread for the tea,' she said. 'And are you all all right?'

She saw Peter.

'Daft soul,' she said. 'Has he been pestering you?'

'That dog got me dinna!' yelled Peter.

Auntie Mona giggled.

'Is that right?' she said.

'Aye!' said Peter. 'What would ye say if I said that dog got me dinna?'

Auntie Mona took out her purse. She held out some pennies to him.

Peter shuffled meekly towards her and took the coins.

'There,' she said. 'Get yourself a pie from Myers and stop pestering people.'

Peter closed his lips tight and shuffled away towards Felling Square.

'Poor daft soul,' said Auntie Mona.

'Aha!' he yelled. 'And what would ye say if I said the best pies is from Dickmans?'

Auntie Mona laughed and said she had to get off. They'd soon be back for their tea. She hurried away.

'Which one was that?' said Margaret.

'Auntie Jan,' said Mary.

'No,' said Catherine. 'Auntie Mona.'

Beside the rocky path, Dandy chased the bees again.

'What *would* you say if Daft Peter knew those things?' said Margaret.

'I'd say it was Daft Question Day,' said Mary.

We looked back over the hundreds of houses towards the graveyard.

Catherine said, 'Maybe Heaven doesn't have to be so big. They said at school that sometime soon the number of people alive will be more than all the people who've ever lived.'

We pondered this while Dandy rushed madly through the foxgloves.

'It's nice to think they're there together, isn't it?' said Mary.

'Yes,' we said.

Dandy trotted home and disappeared. At the gate we smelt the bara brith baking.

'Did you say a prayer for me?' said Mam.

'Yes,' we said.

'And I put daisies on the grave,' said Mary.

'They'd like that.'

She took the bara brith out of the oven and laid it on a wire rack to cool. I sat on the back step with Catherine and we looked out at the immensity of the sky. Margaret sat on the White Chair With A Hundred Holes Like Stars and drew herself and Catherine and Mary flying around Felling's trees. Mary told Mam about Dandy, Daft Peter, Auntie Mona and Auntie Jan. We heard Colin's scooter rattling up Felling Bank and turning into the street. He roared into the garden, and pulled his parka and his helmet off as he came into the house.

Then we all sat at the little table in the bright kitchen. We ate huge slices of the warm bread, sighed at the sweetness of sultanas, caught the melting butter with our tongues, squeezed in tight at the middle of the world.

Counting the Stars

Each year Father O'Mahoney told us about the stars. He told us at the year's end, when the oldest of us were about to leave St John's and go up to St Joseph's. Each time it was the same. He stood in the school hall in his black clothes with the single band of white about his throat to give us his prayers, his congratulations and his warnings. When he spoke of knowledge he made a fist and glared down at the leavers in the front row below him.

'You will come upon those who will tell you everything is knowable,' he said. 'Those who will look into the night and say they can tell you the number of the stars. Turn away from them. It is a blasphemy for man to feign knowledge of what can be known only to God.'

One year one of us, either in mischief or in search of catechismic certainties, was bold enough to raise his hand.

'Father, how many stars can I count before it becomes a sin?'

The priest was silent for a moment.

'It is beyond a hundred that the sin begins to deepen, my son. Beyond a hundred and your soul begins to darken. Beyond a hundred and you take your very life in your hands.'

He paused again, contemplating his answer.

'Yes,' he murmured. 'Beyond a hundred. That's about the time.'

And for ever after, this precise and local doctrine was repeated and became our lore.

On glittering autumn nights, I made a circle of my thumb and forefinger and peered through into the dozens and dozens of stars in that small space. I compared the smallness of this circle with the vastness all around and understood the huge potential of the night for blasphemy and death. My friends and I would tantalise and tempt ourselves when darkness ended our football games and we sprawled on the cold grass and our breath rose in plumes and vapour curled from the exposed skin of our hands and legs.

Ninety, one would begin, pointing upward, passing it on to the next in line. *Ninety-one . . . ninety-two . . . ninety-three . . .* Our fright was disguised with giggles and curses, but we were truly in fear and trembling if ever the boldest among us began to speak the fateful numbers beyond ninety-nine.

As I grew older, of course, and once I'd left St John's myself, I soon saw through this subterfuge: the attempts of an old Irish priest to stifle the liberating effects that education might have on our minds, to keep us in a state of obeisance and fright before his worn-out religion. In my new school, I plunged happily into the intricacies of number and computation. I learned that the earth existed in an obscure corner of an obscure galaxy in what for all we knew might be an obscure universe in a universe of universes. I learned the potential endlessness of all numbers. I knew the numbers of our nearest stars and the distances between them. I peered through binoculars from my bedroom window and saw the stars beyond the stars, and I counted them, and ignored the impossibility of numbering individuals.

'One million,' I whispered. 'Two million . . .'

Sometimes, from his bed three feet away from mine, my brother Colin would whisper and complain.

'What the hell you doing?'

'Nothing. Just counting. Three million. Four million . . .'

It exasperated him. He had dismissed such childish nonsense years ago while I experienced each time the thrill of my transgression. My voice was steady and bold in the small room. I knew by now that it was the smallness of our brains, rather than the wrath of God, that kept our understanding in thrall.

I was fourteen when it was my oldest sister Catherine's turn to leave St John's. At the end of her last day I made sure I was at the garden gate to greet her.

'O'Mahoney's been blathering about the stars,' I said.

'*Father* O'Mahoney,' she said.

I laughed at the word.

'Father! Anyway, don't believe him. I bet he warned you about counting.'

She shrugged.

'It's nonsense. I'll show you tonight.'

That night I waited for the long summer dusk to end and for true darkness to fall. I tiptoed to her room. I shuffled past Mary and Margaret's bed. I woke her and we knelt on her bed and leaned on the windowsill and pressed our faces close to the pane. We heard the gentle breathing of our parents as they slept next door. I began in the lowest corner of the sky, pointing down over the rooftops of our estate to the sky above St Patrick's steeple, and began to count. My finger ticked off the amounts above our small town, leaving untouched the huge expanse of universe beyond. She began to tremble as the numbers mounted.

'Don't,' she whispered.

I held her as she began to pull away. I grinned as I counted more quickly and ran the numbers together in a blur.

'Hundred,' I said at last. 'Hundred and one, hundred and two, hundred and three. See?'

I saw the stars reflected in her eyes, how they shone among her tears. We heard Mary and Margaret stirring. I leaned down and touched the young girls' heads.

'It's nothing,' I whispered. 'Go back to sleep.'

I touched Catherine's head, too.

'Are you all right?' I said.

She didn't answer.

I told her she was too young now, but one day she'd understand.

I tiptoed back to my room.

I lay looking out into the night. I cursed myself.

'Forgive me,' I said into the silence, before descending into my rationalist's dreams.

Soon afterwards, our father became ill. He stayed in his bed. He had time off work. There was trouble in his groin, then in his back, his chest. In the night we heard his baffled exclamations of pain. He was taken to hospital where the speed of his decline simply accelerated. He lay pale-faced on the white bed and stared astonished at us and our mother. He licked his dried-out lips. His voice faded to a whisper: *What the hell's going on?*

They opened him to see what was inside and they quickly closed him again. He was sent back to us with a piece of his lung removed. He told us the worst was over. Their bed was put in the front living-room downstairs. Now the house was filled with the rasping of his breath, Mam's desperately comforting whispers.

'What's wrong?' we asked her.

She shook her head. An infection. Not what had been expected. Nothing. He would get better now.

'What had it been?' we asked.

She shook her head again. Nothing. A mystery. She turned her eyes away.

In the evenings he sat among us in his dressing gown. Often he asked me to rub his back with ointments. The room filled with the scents of Ralgex or Deep Heat while I ran my fingers over his flesh, his ribs and spine, feeling each time how the skin was gathered closer to the bone, and learning how the source of pain each time was more elusive.

He yelped and stiffened and sighed with gratitude.

'That's better, son,' he whispered. 'Rub it all away.'

When nothing worked and it became unbearable, Mam would send Colin or me running down to the Bay Horse for brandy and we knew moments of joy those nights when he was tipsy enough to go beyond the pain and tell us of how it would be once he was well again. We complied in this comforting fiction. We sat in a circle around him and kept our eyes from those of our mother, from the truth that was so dark and deep and obvious beneath the bright surface of her smiles.

The year darkened. All autumn, Mary and Margaret kept being sent away to stay with our grandparents. The doctor and the priest became familiar visitors in the house. Father O'Mahoney would rest his great hand on my head.

'You must pray very hard,' he would tell me, and I would answer, 'Yes, Father,' as he stepped out into the night.

Christmas approached, with sleet and huge dull clouds hanging over everything. Mary and Margaret dropped notes behind the gas fire, requests for presents and for Daddy to be well again. They prepared a card for him: vivid blue night, single perfect five-pointed star shining on the Holy Family. In deeper ignorance than any of us, they scanned the sky and lamented the gloom up there.

'How will he see through that?' they asked. 'How will he ever find his way to us?'

All of us were asked to go to our grandparents for Christmas Day. We sat around Dad's bed eating chocolate and taking sips of his sherry and pulling presents from stockings, then he and Mam kissed us all in turn as we went out.

Colin kept us in order as we took the short walk through the quiet streets. 'They need this special day together,' he explained as we followed him. 'A day of rest to keep him getting better.' We admired the girls' new shoes, the brilliant patent shine on them. We heard distant carols pouring from radios. We smelt Christmas dinners, saw the families behind the windows. Catherine showed us the beautiful long silvery clouds, the moon still shining alongside the sun even though it was day. We entered the other house to huge embraces, pillowcases filled with gifts.

We returned at dusk, when frost glittered like starlight on the pavements. He was sleeping, Mam drowsed in the chair by the bed. The steel sick bowl lay by his pillow. He was pallid, grey-yellow; the pyjama top hung loosely over his bones. He woke up for a moment as Mam whispered about their day together, how joyous he'd been, how he'd loved the food, how he'd asked what time we'd return. He stared at us in amazement, then touched Mam on her arm and asked us, 'Do you understand you're in the presence of one of God's chosen angels?'

Then Boxing Day, and the doctor, and Mary and Margaret sent away again, and Father O'Mahoney as the light failed, blacker than ever in his suit and with the black-fringed stole hanging over his shoulders and the white host in his pocket and the darkness in his eyes. From the front living-room we heard the insistent murmur of Latin, we caught the scent of the anointing oil.

When the priest left, he spanned my head with his hand again, and could say nothing, and I pressed upward to him, searching for the strength and comfort in him.

Then just Dad's breathing, his groans, Mam's eternal comforting.

It was Catherine who heard him die. She was in her bedroom above him. I was somewhere in the house, head ringing with prayers and appeals to God, to Jesus, His mother and all the Saints, to anything that might make things as they were again. She told me years later that she heard the final gasping of his breath below, then silence, nothing, and she knew it was over.

Their bed was removed and his coffin brought in and all the days he lay there I was unable to make myself go in to him. The house teemed with visitors: our boundless relatives; the Legion of Mary; the Knights of St Columba; the Women's League. Father O'Mahoney came time and again. The Brothers of St Vincent de Paul gathered in the garden then poured in from the dark and the house shuddered at their chanting of the rosary. All week Mam sat white-faced, gracious, miraculously calm. Then he was taken away and Colin and I served at the funeral in white robes and we all splashed holy water into the earth after him and chanted the prayers and threw handfuls of dirt and wafted the smoke of incense over him. Afterwards in the crowded house tender words were repeated and repeated. He was at peace now. He would be looking down on us with love. A day would come when all of us would meet again. Aunties tended to us, two of Dad's sisters, the dark-haired identical twins. Mary and Margaret in bright new dresses and their shining new shoes squeezed in at Mam's sides. There were many tears, and some laughter as my father's sisters and brothers talked of his childhood. Then dusk deepened, and one by one and group by group the guests began to take their leave of us.

I was at the back step as the priest came out. The stars had begun to thicken above our town. I felt his great hand on my shoulder.

'Sometimes there can seem to be no light,' he whispered. 'There can seem no sense in it.'

He squeezed me.

'You must pray very hard, my son.'

When he'd gone Colin moved past me into the deeper darkness of the lawn. I went to stand beside him. Soon Catherine came through the threshold behind us. Our faces reflected the light from the house, and we were silvery like moons. We looked over this small place: the house with Mam and her youngest daughters visible in it, the twins moving across the window with trays of food in their hands, the lights and rooftops of this small town, St Patrick's steeple, the lights of the great city beyond and the sky above.

'Why did he die?' asked Catherine.

No answer, silence, nothing.

The world plunged unstoppably through the wilderness.

Ice began to form on our clothes and hair.

I knew from school that we would journey through a meteor storm that night. We waited, close together, until the first of the falling stars appeared. We gasped and pointed and whispered the numbers, but we lost count as the storm intensified and stars cascaded out of the diminishing night.

The Built-up Sole

I was watching myself too much in the mirror. Steve clicked his tongue, his scissors flashed, he cut away yet more of my hair.

'Beware of vanity, boy,' he said. 'One day you'll see the devil at your back.'

I looked through the mirror into Felling Square behind. Late afternoon, November. Brilliant autumn light. The older boys were out there, in their bright shirts, their little jackets, their dark glasses.

'Look at the state of them,' Steve said. 'Look at the nancy boys. You want to end up like that?'

He scissored again. He sucked hard on a cigarette. He glared at me through the glass.

'Do you?' he said.

Then the girls came, strolling past the window. His scissors quickened. He cursed them all, their bangles and beads, tight jeans, short skirts, their thin-soled pointed shoes. I stared and stared, and imagined being out there, until Steve stamped his

22

cigarette out and took his clippers in his fist. I asked if he needed to do this every time and he muttered that it was the only way to get a proper finish. I looked at him: the grubby white tunic buttoned to his throat, the little pot belly, the bulbous nose. I lowered my head for him. It would soon be over. Soon he'd rub the pink glutinous stuff between his palms, spread it over my scalp, comb it through. It would stiffen in seconds, each hair petrified in place.

Steve was one of those barbers with a built-up sole. The boot on his right foot had a four-inch deep black slab below it. Mam said that when Steve was a boy disability was commonplace. He bore the marks of the old diseases and conditions that now were conquered. A training school in Blyth had taken youths with shortened legs and turned them into barbers. When I complained about the clippers, the slippery pink stuff, Steve's beery breath, she used to say,

'Don't be cruel. Think how lucky you are compared with him.'

Old men and obedient boys like me were the ones who went to Steve. Others had their hair lightly trimmed at Crawley's in Low Fell. They went to Gabrielli's in Newcastle and had it styled by Maria or Luigi or Angelo himself.

Time after time I told Mam I was old enough to follow them.

'Not yet,' she'd say. 'Steve needs the custom of those like us. Don't be cruel to him, eh? Not yet.'

It was Simon who was cruel. And Hutchie, of course. As I lowered my head, there was a tapping at the window. It was Hutchie. Simon stood over him. He tottered, leaned on the younger boy. He lifted his right foot and showed the thick block of wood tied with string to his shoe. Steve shoved my head down again, dug the clippers into my neck again.

'Your friends?' he said.

I grunted.

He clippered me again. He brushed the clippings from beneath my collar. He spread the pink stuff on me, combed it through. He pulled the sheet from my throat and wiped his hands on it.

Simon lurched across the window, stepping high then plunging down again.

I handed Steve some coins. He picked some clippings from my collar.

'The hairs of your head are numbered,' he said. 'You must account for each of them on the day of judgement.'

He combed me for the final time. His hands rested on my shoulder.

'Take care, son,' he whispered, then he let me go.

I hurried out to the others and we roared with laughter as we walked into the centre of the square.

At the fountain, I rubbed away the crisp dried dressing. The air was bitter on my temples and neck. Hutchie fingered my stubble.

'Much d'you pay for that?' he said.

He giggled when I told him.

'How bloody much?'

His own hair was filthy and straight. Bits of it stuck out across his ears. I shoved him away. I borrowed Simon's sole and copied his walk.

'I'm Steve,' I laughed. 'Watch out for the nancy boys. Let me stick this pink stuff on your hair.'

As dusk came, the older boys and girls gathered on the benches.

'Look at her,' said Hutchie, peering through the gloom. 'And her. And her and all.'

Our policeman, Sergeant Fox, strode across the square with his hands behind his back. We stamped our cigarettes out.

'Home soon, now, boys,' he told us softly.

He nodded towards the others.

'Don't follow that lot's ways, not yet.'

I looked towards Steve's window. It was a great rectangular glare with his name dark upon it. Inside, he swept the floor, he flicked a duster at the mirror.

'I wish I was older,' I said. 'Don't you?'

'Yes,' said Simon. He tipped his head back. His hair curled across his collar. His breath condensed, rose gently from his face.

'Look at her,' he whispered.

'Her and all,' said Hutchie.

I felt my coarse stubble, my icy skin. I imagined fistfuls of hair, hair flopping across my collar, hair tumbling across my eyes.

Steve took off his white tunic, put a tight-fitting dark coat on. He scooped the money from his cash drawer. He turned off his lights. He hobbled out, and we laughed at his queer undulating stride.

'Let's follow him,' said Hutchie.

'Leave him alone,' I said.

Simon flung his mock sole into a flower bed and led us away. We waited in doorways while Steve called at The Blue Bell's off licence and at Todd's newsagents.

We followed him through the icy mist, through the shadows beyond the High Street towards his bedsit in the new blocks where the terraces had been. We followed the clink of his bottles, the slap of his heavy boot, the click of his light one.

We hesitated on some waste ground.

Simon touched my temple.

'Do you want to come with us?' he said.

I nodded. I held his hair for a second between my fingers.

'You don't know what we'll be up to,' he said.

'I'll come,' I said.

Hutchie laughed.

'Come on, then,' he said. 'He'll be in by now.'

We moved again. Steve's light came on. He came to his window, tugged his curtains together. I stayed close to Simon while Hutchie hurried on.

'Why do you hang about with *him*?' I said.

'He's a laugh,' he said. 'And you wouldn't do what he'll do.'

He held the back of my neck and stared into my eyes.

'Would you?' he said.

I pulled away.

'I don't know,' I said.

He grinned.

'You wouldn't, and you know it.'

We moved on. There were lights in many windows, but no one would be able to see out into the night.

Hutchie looked into Steve's window through the tunnel of his hands.

'He's all alone,' he told us. 'Poor little soul.'

He grinned.

'When I was little I used to be scared of him,' he said.

He turned his face towards the bedsit.

'Cripple,' he whispered. 'Cripple.'

He held his laughter in.

'Let's get him,' said Simon.

They grinned at each other.

'You coming?' said Simon, touching me again. 'Ha. Not you. See what I mean?'

Hutchie giggled. He slapped my bare neck.

'Much d'you say you paid for that?'

They went to the entrance to the block and stepped inside.

I went to Steve's window and peered through the narrow gap where the curtains didn't meet.

Steve was in his chair. There was a beer bottle and a glass on a table before him. He was reading a magazine from Todd's. His discarded boots were on the floor. I saw his little white foot, his stunted toes. He raised his head, listened, lurched to his door. Hutchie came in first. Then Simon kicked the door closed, held Steve from behind, kept his hand across Steve's

27

eyes. He whispered into Steve's ear. Then Hutchie was at the window, grinning out, his face level with mine. He tugged the curtains wider, letting me see everything that he did inside.

Nothing much. He smashed the beer bottle on the wall. He ripped the magazine into little pieces and scattered them on the floor. He pulled Steve's built-up boot on. He spat at Steve. He dug his finger into Steve's cheek and whispered what must have been curses and warnings at him. He shoved his hand into Steve's pocket and took out some coins. Steve didn't struggle. He hung loosely in Simon's arms until he was allowed to fall, and lay there until the boys went out again into the night.

Hutchie shoved the coins into my hand. 'It cost you nowt,' he said. He leaned on Simon and they giggled as they tottered into the night. I waited there. At last Steve came to look out through his hands. There was no way of knowing if he saw me there, or if he knew me. We stared through the glass towards each other for a while. Then the tears began to trickle through his fingers.

I headed back through the darkness towards the square. I made my way through the older girls and boys. Sergeant Fox was at the fountain as I passed. He muttered it was time for home now, wasn't it?

I kept Steve's money in my bedroom. For some time I was thought of as a rebel. I refused to have my hair cut. I said I'd grown beyond all that. Mam asked me to think of poor Steve, but she started to say it was maybe time to go to Crawley's. I wouldn't go. I loved to feel my hair between my fingers, to tug it down towards my collar.

Simon and Hutchie were breaking up. Simon wore a leather jacket and dark glasses. He grew taller, his hair hung in exquisite waves around his face. He spent time with the girls in the square. He turned away if I passed by. Hutchie wandered twitchily on his own, or picked up younger kids to walk with him. His hair bushed out, spiky and uncontrollable. I never met his eye.

Across the square, I saw the limping man in the white tunic, the wall of mirrors, the old men and the boys.

It was almost Christmas when we heard that Steve had gone mad. He'd been in The Blue Bell. He'd gone out into the dark, hobbled to his shop. He kicked the window in with his built-up boot. He climbed inside and smashed the mirrors. He started to tear his shop to bits. By the time Sergeant Fox climbed in to him he was on the floor in a litter of scissors and clippers and broken glass. He was bleeding, foaming at the mouth, gurgling, howling. The policeman held him down. He called to the watching crowd to get some reinforcements.

Next day, the broken glass had been cleared from the pavement, but the shop was full of debris. You could see patches of dried blood. A few boards were nailed where the window had been. Sergeant Fox stood by the door. There was a great white bandage on his right hand and an elastoplast on his cheek. He warned us to keep back for our own protection.

'Yes,' he said. 'The human mind is indeed a mysterious thing.'

As I walked back across the square, Hutchie was with a bunch of little kids. He had Steve's built-up boot on. He was hobbling in circles, grunting, going mad.

'I'm Steve,' he said. 'I'm Steve!'

'Take it off,' I said.

I grabbed him by the throat, made him take it off and give it to me.

Simon was watching, and he smiled at me.

'Your hair,' he said. 'It's coming on nicely.'

The boot dangled from my hand as I left the square. I felt the sullen stubborn weight of its built-up sole. There was nothing I could do, and I flung it into the piles of rubble where the terraces had been.

Steve was taken to St Mary's. Mam said we should visit him there and take some Christmas cake and sherry for him. 'Poor soul,' she called him. 'Poor troubled soul.' She shook her head and raised her eyes to Heaven. 'What can have caused all that?'

She'd heard that his shop was to be sold, that Crawley intended to take over.

'Will you go back then?' she asked.

I shrugged.

She clicked her tongue and pulled my ragged hair.

'Look at this mess,' she said. 'Please get it cut for Christmas.'

That Saturday, I put Steve's money in my pocket. I went to Newcastle. I sat in the line of gleaming chairs in Gabrielli's. My hair was washed by Maria. It was trimmed and styled and left to curl over my collar by the gentle hands of Angelo himself.

The Subtle Body

I fell in love with Theresa as I came back from kissing the cross.

It was Good Friday afternoon. St Patrick's church was packed. Babies squealed. Old women whimpered in grief. The place reeked of incense and sweat and beery breath. The priests' voices droned in prayer and wobbled in song. They went on and on about death and Hell and gloom. The day darkened and darkened and darkened. A hailstorm roared in from the North Sea.

I squirmed on my hard seat. Never again. Never again.

I was with Mick Flannery. He'd gone off to train to be a priest when he was eleven. Two months ago they'd sent him back, and he was quickly making up for lost time. It was Mick who spotted Theresa. We were shuffling to the altar. The choir was groaning through 'O Sacred Heart'.

'Corduroy suit. Black hair,' he hissed. 'Lovely.'

She was on her way back, black mantilla draped across her head.

'An angel,' he moaned. 'Who is she?'

A mystery. I dipped my head as Father O'Mahoney held out the cross. I kissed the great black nail that pierced Christ's feet.

Going back I saw her a few rows beyond our own. Her eyes were piously downcast.

The priests said that Christ had begun his voyage through death, that like all of us he would rise again, that like all of us he would return in more glorious form.

I kept turning.

She raised her dark eyes to me, and my heart was hers.

Afterwards, we waited in the dusk beneath St Patrick's statue until she came. She was with a girl I knew, Mary or Maria, who lived out Heworth way. We followed them towards Felling Square then on to Watermill Lane where heavy trees grew from the verges and yellow streetlights shone down through the spring leaves.

'What can we do?' said Mick.

I started to run.

Maria held Theresa tight.

'What you after?' she asked.

'Saw you in church,' I said to Theresa. I gagged and gaped. 'Never seen anybody so beautiful.'

'She's Theresa,' said Maria. 'My cousin. She's from Winlaton.'

'Come out with me,' I said.

Mick struck a match behind me.

'She's come to be with me,' said Maria.

'All of us,' I said. 'You and all. Mick and all.'

They huddled together and whispered and giggled, then Theresa came in close. Her corduroy on the back of my hand, her scent, the sweetness of her breath.

'Tomorrow,' she whispered. 'Same time. Here.'

And they were gone, heels clacking through the shadows of the trees.

The back of my hand was tingling. My spirit was soaring.

'Thanks be,' Mick said.

'Amen. Amen.'

Dad was still alive then. He told me I was a member of the most privileged generation the world had ever seen. There'd be nothing I couldn't do. Nothing must hold me back. We used to stand together in the garden and he talked about the war, how it had stifled his own generation. He said a time of great liberation had arrived. He understood the doubts that I was prey to: the problems of my faith, the complexity of my young body, the yearnings and confusions of my liberated mind. He said there were temptations and possibilities he had no experience of.

Mam used to cry when I questioned the faith. But he used to whisper, 'Find your own way. Go as far as you need.'

He'd hold me close.

'Just don't leave us behind. You'll need us waiting here with our love.'

Then he'd ask about books, and we'd start to smile. He knew that the library had begun to overcome the church.

The library was a prefabricated place on a green beside the square. I took out armfuls of Hemingway and Lawrence and forgotten names from the Recommended New Novels section. I pored in excited confusion through *The Waste Land* and *The Cantos*. I learned Dylan Thomas and Stevie Smith by heart. I plundered the shelves of the paranormal. I devoured surveys of the occult, read tantalising accounts of spontaneous combustion, the aura, teleportation, poltergeists and human vanishings. I took home books on yoga and propped them on the bedroom floor as I attempted the Plough or the Lotus or teetered upside-down on my head. I squatted between the beds, meditated, and attempted to reach some higher plane.

I kept reading about the body's subtlety: there was the thing of bones and the thing of spirit; in between was an astral body with elements of both these forms. This body could be inhabited by adepts, who travelled in the astral plane above the material world. I wanted to do this. I wanted to learn the necessary mantras, to submit to arcane disciplines. But the references were coy and confusing, gushing descriptions, no instruction.

Then I discovered the books of T. Lobsang Rampa, my exotic counterpart, my guide. He was a Tibetan monk forced into exile by the barbaric Chinese. His map of Lhasa in *The Third Eye* was an exalted version of Felling. I imagined walking past the Potala Palace as I walked past Felling Square, loitering in Norbu Linga as I loitered in Felling Park, gazing down towards the Kyi Chu River as I gazed towards the Tyne.

Lobsang taught me that there were no secrets. Imagination

was the only key. With thumping heart I read his words, so thrilling, so intimate:

As you lie alone upon your bed, keep calm. Imagine that you are gently disengaging from your body. Imagine that you are forming a body the exact counterpart of your physical body, and that it is floating above the physical, weightlessly. You will experience a slight swaying, a minute rise and fall. There is nothing to be afraid of. As you keep calm you will find that gradually your now-freed spirit will drift until you float a few feet off. Then you can look down at yourself, at your physical body. You will see that your physical and your astral bodies are connected by a shining silver cord which pulsates with life. Nothing can hurt you so long as your thoughts are pure.

Dad was with me in the living room as I read this. He smiled at the three eyes and the snowy mountains on the cover. He told me as he so often did about Burma, the wet heat and stench of the jungle, the awful fear of the Japanese.

'I saw the Himalayas once,' he said. 'Went with a mate on leave. Travelled north for days. Came one night to a station in the middle of nowhere. We sat on the platform, waiting. Lots of Indians beside us with blankets pulled over their heads. Over the line there was a fire burning and they were playing flutes and a girl was dancing. I kept thinking of your mother, of Felling, getting home again. Kept nodding off, dreaming of being here, certain I was here, then jerking awake again. The sun came up and straight away it was blazing hot and glaring and the fields were shimmering and the line was shining bright. There they were, the Himalayas, out past everything. Icy white and still and beautiful. They just drew your eyes to them and held them. Then the train came and chaos started and we were heading back again.'

He smoked and coughed and smiled again.

'Always said I'd go back there. Tibet, maybe. Nepal . . . Maybe you will, though.'

I went on reading.

If you imagine it strongly enough you can do it.

'Aye. You know there's more than this. Maybe you will.'

I couldn't do it. Too much disturbance. Not enough purity. Not enough imagination. Night after night I tried. Often I felt the minute rise and fall. I was on the point of breaking free. I imagined looking down upon Felling, lights arranged in rows along the streets, dark patches of parks and gardens, the river's gleam, all of Tyneside glittering in the night. I imagined travelling to Tibet itself, to the snowy peaks, the eagles, the palaces, the fluttering prayer flags. I imagined the shining cord stretching back to the bony body on the bed. But each night I lay surrounded only by the known and the familiar: the small house, the darkness, Dad's snoring, one of my sisters murmuring in her sleep.

And on Good Friday Theresa disturbed my imaginings: her dark hair and eyes, her sweetness and her breath, and my anticipation of tomorrow.

Mick and I stood beneath the trees. We breathed smoke through the mist towards the lights.

'Tell me about the Fathers,' I said.

'Why's it always that you want to know?'

'Were there things you can't talk about?'

'Things?'

'Secrets. Things they taught you. Things they showed you.'

'We did Latin all the time. They told us about Africa and malaria. They went on and on about Hell. They showed us how to lie in bed in an attitude of prayer. We had to contemplate our end and rise above the flesh.'

'And did you?'

'All we talked about was girls. All we imagined was girls.'

He had the wildness in his eyes that had come back from the Fathers with him.

'They asked about our dreams. They searched our lockers, read our letters. They were evil, man.'

The girls didn't come. We scanned the houses, looked for the Sacred Heart medallions in the doorlights that showed where Catholics were. We cursed and blasphemed. Then there was a door ajar, a crack of light inside the frame, music playing. We stepped through the gate.

Mick gripped my arm.

'You have the pretty one,' he said. 'I saw the way she looked at you. I'll have the other. Right?'

I peered through the doorlight, past the medallion's silhouette. From inside came the singing of Smokey Robinson and the Miracles.

'Must be them,' he said. He rapped on the door.

Hurrying feet and laughter, then Maria, peering out.

'What you doing?' she asked.

'You said you'd come.'

'How d'you know we wouldn't?'

'We waited.'

'And we're not worth waiting for?'

'Let's come in.'

Theresa came, stood in the hall.

'They want to come in,' laughed Maria.

She sniggered, then let us through. I saw Christ exposing his heart for us. I smelt Theresa, felt her hand brush against mine.

'Nobody in?' said Mick.

Maria laughed.

'They're at the vigil.'

We drank sherry that tasted like altar wine. The girls sat on a sofa and Mick and I on deep chairs. Smokey finished and the Temptations slapped down on to the turntable. There was a statue of the Virgin Mary on the mantelpiece. Plaster angels flew across the walls. We tapped our cigarettes relentlessly on the rims of ashtrays. Theresa talked about Winlaton, in the hills beyond Felling. So rough, lads fighting in the streets all the time. She'd dreamed for weeks of coming here.

'But I can't stay long,' she said, and she gazed into my eyes.

Mick left me and sat on the sofa with his arm around Maria. Theresa smiled and turned the light off and came to me and we kissed.

'I hoped you'd come,' she whispered.

We kissed again.

'Don't be scared,' she said.

I imagined floating through the room, seeing the two of us tangled below me on the armchair.

'Keep calm,' whispered Theresa.

I ran my hands across her.

'Not too far,' she whispered.

We lay sighing.

'I'm glad you were in the church,' she whispered. 'You believe in it?'

'It?'

'God. Sin. Angels. Hell and Heaven. Soul and body. All that. The Cross. That He came back from death and ascended into Heaven.'

'No.'

'Me neither.'

'You like my body?' she whispered.

I sighed and my heart raced.

'Yes. I believe in astral bodies, as well,' I said.

'Astral bodies?'

'They're like souls. You float out of yourself and travel in the astral plane. It's true. All it takes is imagination.'

She sniggered.

'Imagine it,' I said. 'Close your eyes. Imagine that we're rising together from the chair, that we can look down at ourselves. Imagine it. It can happen. It can really happen.'

'I'm floating,' she murmured.

For a moment it seemed true. We felt Lobsang's swaying, we began to rise from the chair. We held each other tight and kissed. Then Maria called.

'Hey. You two.' She giggled. 'Come back to the real world. Time to go.'

We went into the night, all four of us. Theresa pressed against me as we walked.

I told her about Lobsang, Tibet, the Himalayas, the astral plane.

Our breath glowed and thickened beneath the lights. Our lips were tender. We hid in the shadows as families moved past us from the vigil. Soon Maria said they'd have to go. Theresa drew me into a heavy overhanging hedge and we kissed again.

I walked with Mick through the mist to Felling Square. I could still smell her, feel her skin, hear her breath in my ear. Mick trembled and skipped in excitement.

'Wow,' he kept saying. 'Wow. How far'd you go?' he said.

I smiled.

'Far enough.'

'Aye. Far enough.'

We smoked a cigarette beside the fountain then went our separate ways into the gloom.

'You weren't at the vigil,' said Mam as I entered the house.

I turned my eyes down.

'Your faith's your most precious thing,' she said.

'I know that.'

I felt sure they must catch the smell of Theresa that surrounded me. I stared at our statues and angels. A rosary lay in a little heap on the mantlepiece.

'I was talking about your Tibetan bloke in the club,' said Dad. 'It seems he's a Kerry man that's not set foot outside Ireland.'

'I've seen that. Nobody's certain, though.'

He smiled.

'He's the real thing to you.'

'Yes.'

That night as I slept I travelled over Felling. Theresa raised her arms to welcome me. Our bodies mingled like breath in mist, like angels are supposed to, like astral bodies must.

Easter Sunday morning: the empty tomb, the risen body, the defeat of death, the resurrection of us all. We wore spring clothes and sunlight poured through the windows. Mick was at my side. Close by was Theresa, her eyes so warm each time I turned to her.

The priest held out the body and blood. We lowered our eyes and Mick muttered about Maria. At the altar rail I knelt by Theresa.

'We'll go off on our own,' she whispered. 'We'll leave the others.'

She opened her mouth, she waited for the bread.

'Yes,' I hissed.

We tilted our heads back, closed our eyes, waited to have Christ's body pressed to our tongues.

I knelt afterwards with my head bowed in thanksgiving. I told Mick he should take Maria somewhere on his own. He grinned.

'Aye,' he whispered. 'Then get together later, eh? See where we got to.'

She waited for me in the courtyard. We sidled through the released congregation. We were almost clear when someone tapped me on the shoulder. I turned and there was Dad, smiling at us.

'Who's your friend?' he asked.

'Theresa,' I said. 'Maria's cousin. She's from Winlaton.'

He shook her hand. I stood speechless. He gently laughed, gripped my shoulder, at once holding me and pushing me away.

'Go on, then,' he said. 'On your way, son.'

We held hands on the High Street and moved across the square. Such changes: high thin drifting clouds, immaculate light. We walked up Felling Bank, densely-packed houses on either side. Children squealed in hidden gardens. I led her to Windy Ridge, sloping terraced street with allotments in front and huge playing fields beyond. Scents of wood smoke from gardeners' fires, sun on bare earth, early flowers. Men bending, touching buds, talking with each other over flower beds and vegetable plots. Sun glinting on the greenhouses. Theresa said it was so beautiful here, like somewhere foreign. There were families walking through the fields, boys engrossed in football games. I pointed down to the roof of my home, to Maria's place, to St Patrick's steeple. We traced the gleaming river through the banks of the city to the dark sea. The horizon was dead still, dead clear. I asked if she read and she said she loved modern poetry, French novels, she wanted to know about the

Russians. She said that one day she'd write novels of her own, and not about Winlaton. I told her about Stevie Smith and Lawrence. I said she must read *The Third Eye*, she must learn of Lobsang, his family, his education, how his occult powers were awakened. We talked of the wideness of the world, the narrowness of our homes. We passed the remnants of the abandoned colliery, the broken concrete gun emplacement left from the war. We took a path that led from the fields into the Heather Hills. Wild daffodils. Bracken and fern unfurling. Long strings and clusters of spawn in the ponds. The yellow buds of gorse, the white of hawthorn.

We lay on a grassy slope and looked down over everything. We lay face upward side by side and watched the clouds drifting. Invisible larks were singing high above.

'We can imagine anything,' I said.

We kissed each other.

'We can go anywhere,' she said.

We kissed and kissed. We held each other, subtle body and subtle body. We rocked and swayed and lifted and fell, and we began to leave ourselves, entangled there together in the sunlight on the grass.

Where Your Wings Were

For a long time after Barbara died, Mam used to pull my shoulders forward, kiss me, and slip her fingers beneath my shoulder-blades.

'You as well,' she'd whisper. 'Just like Barbara, you as well. This is where your wings were. You left them behind when you came here. But be good, and you'll have them back again, one day.'

Barbara was an angel. One of those that God takes early. She was too good to stay here long. She died in infancy, flew straight into God's arms.

At night I tried to imagine her there. I lay in my bed, closed my eyes, tried to dream of her. I told myself that if I did see her, then it wouldn't be dreaming. It would be real. I whispered her name: 'Barbara. Little sister, little angel. Let me see you again.' But it wasn't to be. With my eyes closed or with my eyes open, all I could see was the darkness spreading all around.

As I grew older, and could feel the goodness leaving me, I tried to pray to Barbara, but the words appeared to go nowhere, and they brought me no comfort. Often I fingered my own shoulder-blades and tried to imagine my wings, tried to imagine the feathers, bones and muscles known only to angels. But my fingers encountered my skin, my flesh, my bone: a simple human shape, nothing more. I searched my memory, tried to remember being there myself, so that I might try harder to return. I retreated, went back and back, remembered further, further, tried to imagine being inside my mother, then the time that preceded being inside my mother. But I could go no further than when I was an infant of two, maybe three, certainly before Barbara came. My first memory was nothing of note, just me sitting in a pushchair staring up at Mam, and Dad at her side. I believe we're in the garden, we've just come through the gate. My parents are so tall, so dark, silhouetted against the blazing sun. I see Mam lean towards me, smiling. 'Look at him,' she says, and I hear their gentle laughter. 'You all right, my little angel?' she asks. I feel her light touch on my cheek, hear the first words I remember, naming me as an angel.

Before that moment, it is as if there's nothing. I do not exist. Trying to go back only emphasises my going forward. I become older. And as a boy, as I grew older, I felt myself heading further and further towards a terrible dark.

It was painful to lie there failing to imagine Barbara, with my parents sleeping in the room next door, and to feel the time of dreams approaching. There seemed to be nothing I could do about these dreams. I didn't want them, I didn't encourage them. I didn't even have to imagine them. They just came out of the night, out of my skull. They came at me, night after night after night.

I confessed the dreams. At church, I knelt in front of the screen and told Father O'Mahoney about them. He was an old man with a gentle Irish voice that never seemed to criticise anything. I knew he must have heard everything before, but I wanted him to get angry, to shout at me, to warn me of terrible punishments. But he just listened and whispered,

'Yes . . . Oh, dear now . . . Yes . . .'

And then he forgave me, told me to pray for purity, and gave me a penance of Our Fathers, Hail Marys, Glory Bes. It was too easy. Even as I said the penance, kneeling at the altar rail, I knew it would happen again, and I wanted to be punished for it properly, before it became worse.

The dreams of course were about women and girls, about any woman or any girl who had caught my eye during the day.

In the effort to displace these dreams, and to supplement the penances of Father O'Mahoney, I spent many of these nights bringing to mind the day of Barbara's death. Late winter, an unblemished morning, sun streaming in at my window, a chorus of songbirds, silence in the house. Still early, 7 a.m. The day before me stretching endless and unused and filled with hope. And then movement, Mam rising, her awful, awful cry. Our poorly sister wouldn't wake, couldn't wake, was already gone to God. Our mother pursued her, called after her, begged her, gripped our sister in her arms and refused to relinquish her. Colin, Catherine and I gathered at the fringes, useless. A whole morning of prayer and protest and lamentation, till such silence, and despite the sunlight such darkness, fell again. The doctor was allowed to confirm our sister's death, Father O'Mahoney to pray over her. We stumbled from the corners, Mam let us and Dad into her arms, and we wept together and held our cold and long-gone little sister in our useless arms.

The dreams changed. One night my head was filled with a kind of fluttering. I turned towards it and saw an angel landing in my dark. She came towards me, floating rather than walking. She was clothed only in white fire, and her wings stood high behind her, covered in pure white feathers, like those of doves. Through the fire I could see her body, shaped like any woman's, but more beautiful than any woman's. Without speaking, she came to me and I felt her fire all over and inside me. I lay stunned, watching her wings beating gently above us, pure white against the dark.

I told Father O'Mahoney. He listened in silence. Then there was concern in his voice.

'The tricks of the Devil,' he said. 'They will adopt the most exquisite of shapes. Resist them all. Be firm.'

I said my penances. But I was far gone. I knew that my angel would come again, that again she would be wonderful, the most wonderful thing I'd known. Night after night she came to wrap me in her fire, and I welcomed her, embraced her, though I knew she was leading me to Hell.

One night, after she'd been with me for hours, her wings began to beat more quickly and I felt myself being lifted. I held on tight, gazed into her perfect face as we began to fly through the gentle winds of the dark. She kept looking down at me, smiling to reassure me. We travelled for an age, until the dark began to change and we entered a pink dawn that slowly changed to white until the light itself was her fire, and she was so absorbed by it that I could no longer see her. I knew she was there only by feeling her tight in my arms, and by the continued rhythmic beating of her wings. I looked from side to side, wanting to see where we were, but there was only the fire on all sides, going on for ever.

I woke in my crumpled bed. There was frost on the window, snow outside. I closed my eyes tight, wanting the angel again, but I was awake, it was ordinary daylight, and she was gone.

I didn't confess it. I told myself it was just a dream, nothing to do with becoming bad. I just told the old dreams, the old women and girls. Father O'Mahoney said, 'Remember that the body is God's temple, and each of us is forever in God's thoughts.'

The next time, it started like snow falling, a thousand flakes falling from the darkness, each flake a glowing white flame. Then I saw the wings, and beneath the wings the bodies, each one a woman's, but more beautiful than any woman's. A whole flight of angels landed in my dark.

The angel I knew came to me first. Then the others one by one came to join her, until there were a thousand angels with me, and wherever I turned was filled with their white fire, their tender faces, their brilliant bodies, their beating wings.

We went together, all of us, through the winds of the dark, a fiery swarm with me at the centre, until we entered the pink again and then the white. They peeled away from me there, leaving me the one blemish in all that white. I threw my arms out frantically, striking wings and faces and hair, until my hand was taken and the angel drew me towards her and laid her arm across my shoulder.

'Don't worry,' she whispered, and I could tell by the way she spoke that she was smiling. 'There's someone to see you.'

She took my hands and stretched them out into the brightness. My fingertips encountered skin, hair, eyes, a tender cheek. I felt the lips part, felt breath breaking into laughter.

'Barbara,' I gasped. 'Barbara.'

I reached down, I lifted her, and at her back I felt the quick fluttering of her own small wings. She put her arms around my neck and kissed me and spoke my name.

'Oh, Barbara,' I gasped.

So much more I wanted to say. So much more I wanted to cry out. But I became speechless. I could only hold her, feel her as happy and tiny as she always was, feel the life continuing to burn and sparkle in her.

'You see?' she said, and her voice was filled with delight. 'You see? I'm all right. Everything's all right.'

Then she was gone, suddenly, flying out into the light and I knew there was no way to follow her.

'You see?' the angel whispered. 'You see?'

'But how . . . ?' I said. 'How?'

She pressed a finger to my lips.

'Come with me,' she said. 'But never say a word.'

We moved forward, and the white fire burned even more

49

brightly, so brightly that I had to close my eyes against it. When we stopped, she whispered, 'Listen.'

I could hear nothing, only my own breathing and the beating of my heart.

'Listen.'

I started to ask what I should listen for, but then I heard it. Further into the fire, someone else was breathing. Long breaths in and long breaths out, filled with low groans, soft rattling and whistling sounds.

'Hear it?'

'Yes.'

She turned me away, and we went back, to where I could open my eyes again.

'What was it?' I asked.

'That was God, fast asleep. He'll wake up soon. Hold on tight.'

Back we came through the pink and the black, and into my room's darkness where we came to rest. She giggled like Barbara had, and held me at arm's length, preparing to leave.

'Don't go,' I said.

'Everyone will wake up soon,' she said.

'When can I come back again?' I asked.

She touched my cheek and smiled and shook her head.

'One day,' she said. 'When you have your wings again.'

And for the last time she stayed with me, and the white fire that did not burn spread far into me, making me understand how it feels to be angelic. Then she was gone, diminishing to a snowflake, disappearing into the dark . . .

That day Mam did again what she so often did. She pulled my shoulders forward and kissed me.

'You're the bright one this morning,' she said.

I laughed.

I let her slip her fingers beneath my shoulder-blades.

'Where my wings were,' I said. 'Where they'll be again.'

She held me close.

'It's true,' she said. 'Even though you're growing up so fast you have to keep on knowing that it's true.'

I reached up and for the first time slipped my fingers beneath her own shoulder-blades.

'You as well,' I told her.

'Yes, me as well. All of us. Barbara, you, me, all of us. Everybody.'

And then we were silent, and we felt for a moment the fire within us burning, until Dad came in, and we giggled, imagining together the white feathers rising from his hairy back and beyond his balding head.

It was the first time I had asked Father O'Mahoney anything, and it was the first time he became angry.

'If we're like this when we're in God's thoughts,' I said. 'What are we like when we're in his dreams?'

His hand struck the thin screen between us. He shouted at my blasphemy and gave me five decades of the rosary to say. I didn't say them, though. I knew that God slept, that even angels weren't always good, that I'd have my wings back one day, and that dreams were only dreams.

Acknowledgements

These stories, other than **The Built-up Sole**, were published in *Counting Stars* (Hodder Children's Books). They were previously published/broadcast as follows:

The Middle of the World, *Pretext* (EAS Publishing);
Counting the Stars, *Northern Stories 6* (Arc Publications);
BBC Radio 4. **The Built-up Sole**, *Biting Back*, (Iron Press).
Where Your Wings Were, BBC Radio 4.

The extracts on pages 35 and 36 from *The Third Eye* by T. Lobsang Rampa are used with kind permission from the estate of Sarah Anna Rampa.

Also by David Almond

SKELLIG

Michael was looking forward to moving house. It was all going to be wonderful. But now his baby sister's ill, his parents are frantic and Doctor Death has come to call. Michael feels helpless.

Then he steps into the crumbling garage . . .

What is this thing beneath the spiders' webs and dead flies? A human being, or a strange kind of beast never seen before? The only person Michael can confide in is Mina. Together, they carry the creature out into the light, and Michael's world changes forever . . .

Winner of the Whitbread Children's Book of the Year Award and the Carnegie Medal.

'Gripping, beautifully and brilliantly written . . . Everyone is raving about this unforgettable book.' *The Sunday Times*

'David Almond's lyrical tale of the angel Skellig is written with delicacy and restraint, and tells a story of love and faith with exquisite, heart-fluttering tenderness. It is an extraordinarily profound book, no matter how old the reader.' *Chair of the Whitbread Judges*

KIT'S WILDERNESS

In Stoneygate there was a wilderness, an empty space between the houses and the river where the ancient coal pit had once been. In the wilderness Kit met Askew, with his wild dog, Jax. Askew – who ran the game called Death.

The wilderness where Kit begins to confront death – and life . . .

Winner of the Smarties Prize and the Michael L. Printz Award.

'You can feel the chill from the ghosts that haunt its pages. An essential read from an original voice in children's books.' *The Daily Telegraph*

'Establishes Almond as the most exciting new voice in children's books this decade.' *Literary Review*

'Dangerous, exciting, always absorbing.' *The Independent*

HEAVEN EYES

It's easy. Running away from Whitegates. Erin and her running-away friend January do it all the time. But this time they're going down river. This time they might never come back. This time they're looking for a tiny corner of Paradise.

How could they imagine that what they'd find there would be Heaven Eyes? Heaven Eyes. This girl who should have drowned at sea, this girl rescued from the mud. This girl with a secret history only Grampa knows. And he isn't telling . . .

'David Almond understands the joy and fear of being alive better than most – *Heaven Eyes* is a mysterious gift of a novel.' *The Times*

'Another superb novel from this award-winning author.' *Children's Book News*

Also by David Almond

SECRET HEART

Joe Maloney is out of place in this world. His mother wants him to be a man, and he can't be that. His school wants him to stop truanting, and he can't do that. His one friend, Stanny Mole, wants to teach him how to kill, and he can't learn that. Joe's mind is always somewhere else: on the weird creatures he sees around him, on the songs and whispers he hears on the air. Everybody laughs at Joe Maloney.

And then a tiger comes for him, and leads him out into the night, and nothing in Joe Maloney's world is ever the same again.

'This gripping book will enrich your soul and fire your imagination.' *The Daily Telegraph*

'*Secret Heart* is his best book yet.' *Literary Review*